Take AWAY the A

Other Enchanted Lion titles by Michaël Escoffier and Kris Di Giacomo:
My Dad Is Big & Strong, BUT...: A Bedtime Story
Brief Thief
Me First!
The Day I Lost My Superpowers

www.enchantedlionbooks.com

First published in 2014 by Enchanted Lion Books,
67 West Street, 317A, Brooklyn, NY 11222
Copyright © 2014 by Michaël Escoffier for text
Copyright © 2014 by Kris Di Giacomo for illustrations
Copyright © 2014 by Enchanted Lion Books

ISBN 978-1-59270-156-8

Printed by RR Donnelley Asia Printing Solutions Ltd.
Fourth Printing, April 2017

Take AWAY the A

By Michaël Escoffier

Illustrated by Kris Di Giacomo

An
ALPHABEAST
of a book!

ENCHANTED LION BOOKS
NEW YORK

Without the

A

the BEAST is the BEST.

Without the

B

the BRIDE
goes for
a RIDE

Without
the

the CHAIR has HAIR.

Without the

D

DICE are ICE.

Without the

E

BEARS stay behind BARS.

Without the

the SCARF
hides a SCAR.

Without the

G

the GLOVE
falls in LOVE.

Without
the

H

THREE
climb a
TREE.

Without
the

I

STAIRS
lead to the
STARS.

Without the J

Without the

K

Without the

L

PLANTS
wear
PANTS.

Without the M

the FARM is too FAR.

Without the
N

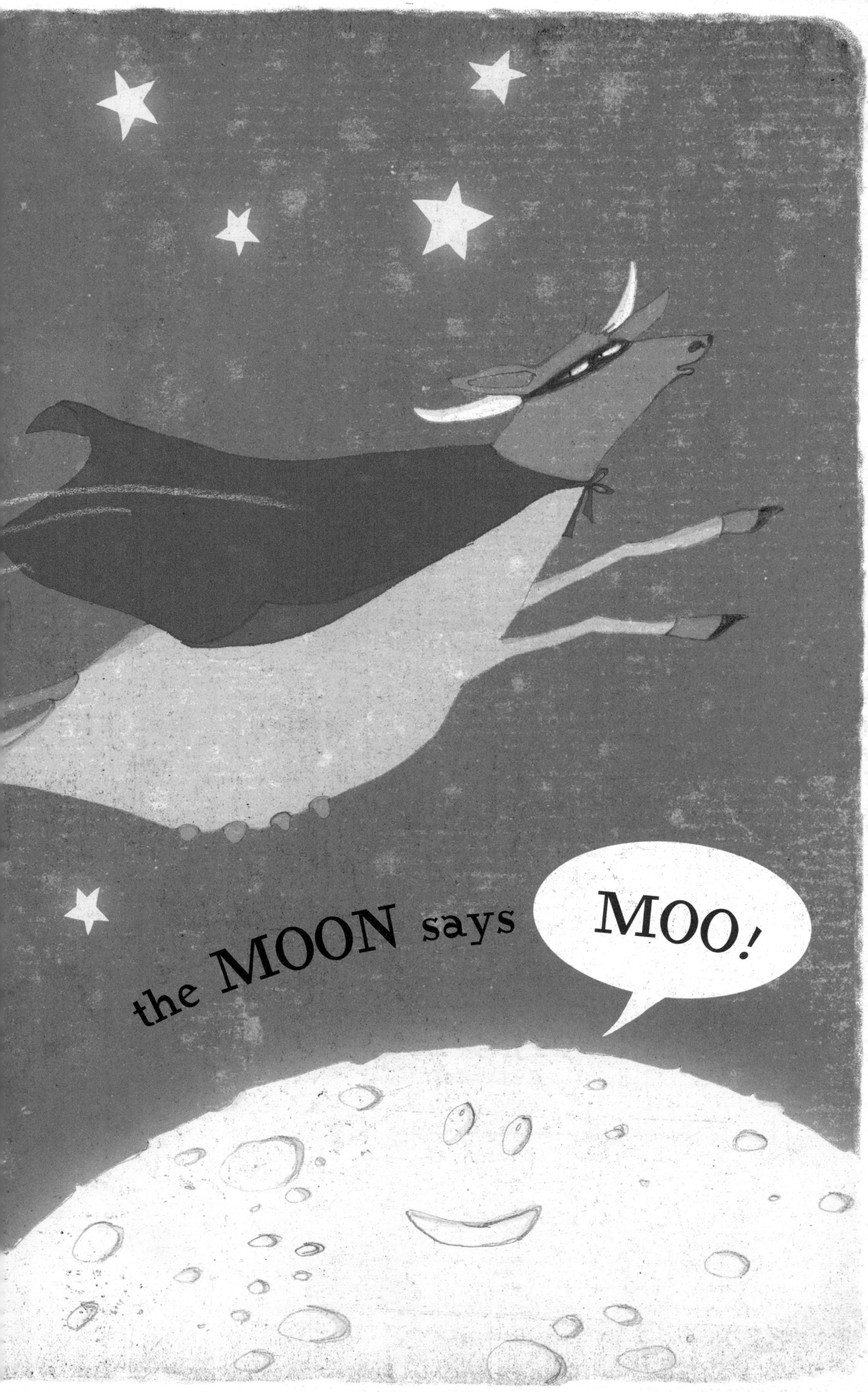
the MOON says
MOO!

Without the

O

FOUR wear FUR.

Without the
P

the **PLATE**
is too **LATE.**

Without the

the FAQIR
goes to the FAIR.

Without the

R

the CRAB
hails a CAB.

Without the S

SNOW falls NOW.

BOATS carry BOAS.

Without
the **U**

my AUNT
is an ANT.

Without the **V**

SEVEN are SEEN.

Without
the
W

the WITCH
has an ITCH.

Without
the

FOXES
are
FOES.

Without the

Y

Without the

we cannot sing our ABC's!

BEAST STAIRS

BRIDE JAM

CHAIR

DICE MONKEY

PLANTS

BEARS FARM

SCARF

GLOVE MOON

THREE FOUR